MAR

W9-BFG-806

D-90

Mr. Floop's Lunch

Mr. Floop's Lunch

c. 1

by MATT NOVAK

ORCHARD BOOKS   NEW YORK

Orchard Books, A division of Franklin Watts, Inc.
387 Park Avenue South, New York, NY 10016

Manufactured in the United States of America. Printed by General Offset Co., Inc. Bound
by Horowitz / Rae. Book design by Mina Greenstein. The text of this book is set in
16 pt. Usherwood Medium. The illustrations are pencil and watercolor reproduced in full color.
10 9 8 7 6 5 4 3 2 1

Library of Congress Cataloging-in-Publication Data
Novak, Matt. Mr. Floop's lunch.
Summary: Mr. Floop gives all of his lunch away to other creatures before finding someone to share
with him. [1. Sharing—Fiction.   2. Animals—Fiction]   I. Title.   PZ7.N867Mr   1990   [E]
89-22963   ISBN 0-531-05826-3   ISBN 0-531-08426-4 (lib. bdg.)

To Amanda and Noelle

ON a day too beautiful to stay inside, Mr. Floop packed a delicious lunch and took it to the park.

When he found a nice spot, he opened his
bag and took out a soft, warm roll. Mr. Floop
loved rolls.

A bird perched on the bench.
"Would you like a bit of roll?" asked Mr.
Floop, and he gave some crumbs to the bird…

and to all the other birds.

When the roll was gone, the birds flew
away.

Mr. Floop reached into his bag again and pulled out a string of juicy sausages.

A small dog trotted over to the bench.
"I know what you want," said Mr. Floop, and
he gave some sausage to the dog...

and to all the other dogs.

When the sausages were gone the dogs ran
away.

Mr. Floop took some crunchy peanuts out of the bag.

A squirrel crawled down the branch of a
tree. Mr. Floop fed a peanut to the squirrel...

and to all the other squirrels.

When the peanuts were gone
the squirrels ran away.

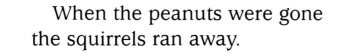

Mr. Floop took a bottle of milk from his bag
and poured himself a nice cool cupful.

A tiny kitten jumped onto the bench and purred very loudly. Mr. Floop looked at the kitten, and then he looked all around. There didn't seem to be any others.

"Well," he said, "maybe just a little." And he gave some milk to the kitten...

and to all the other kittens.

When the milk was gone, the kittens ran away. Mr. Floop sighed. He'd given his bread to the birds, his sausages to the dogs, his peanuts to the squirrels, and his milk to the kittens.

He was very hungry.

Mr. Floop was still hungry when a woman
came by carrying a picnic basket.
"Excuse me," she said. "May I sit here?"

"Please do," said Mr. Floop.

"Thank you," said the woman. "This is my favorite bench." She sat down next to him.

"Yes, it is nice," said Mr. Floop.

"I come here every day and share my lunch with the animals," she said. "I wonder where they are."

"I don't think they're hungry," said Mr. Floop.

"Really?" said the woman.

"Not anymore," he answered.

Then she saw Mr. Floop's empty bag. She smiled.

"Would you like to share my lunch?" she asked.

"I suppose I could eat a bite or two," Mr. Floop said.

"I don't like to eat alone," the woman said,
and she handed Mr. Floop a soft, warm roll.

"Thank you," he said. "I love rolls."

"And I like sharing lunch."

```
E Nov c.1
Novak, Matt.
Mr. Floop's lunch
```